Disclaimer and Terms of Use:

The Author and Publisher have strived to be as accurate and complete as possible in the creation of this book. While all attempts have been made to verify information provided in this publication, the Author and Publisher assume no responsibility for errors, omissions or contrary interpretation of the subject matter herein. Any perceived slights of specific persons, peoples, or organizations are unintentional.

This book is for informational purposes only and is not intended for use as a source of legal, business, medical or financial advice. All readers are advised to seek services of competent professionals in legal, business, medical and finance fields.

Editor: Corinne Casazza, corinnecasazza@gmail.com

Graphic Designer of Cover: Marissa Langdon

Ghost Writer: DIY Entertainment

First Edition, January 6th, 2019

Barnes & Noble

Dedication

To: My Husband Chris, Zoey, and Luke

Another huge thank you to:
Laura, Staci, Mike B., Ashley, Ian, Grandma Ruth, My Parents, Mackenzie, Amy P., Amy W., and Natalie.

I've written at the end of the book, long dedications to all of you! Take a moment to read them; you guys helped me through so much. A simple mention in the beginning isn't enough!

Preface

The idea to write a book about my son and our journey together, started in the most unlikely places. I wanted to start a nonprofit charity to help families with financial needs that have to go in and out of Boston, MA all the time. While speaking with someone about this idea, they looked at me and said, you should really write a book. This idea was amazing, but I put it on the back burner and continued with life. As I started talking to more and more people, they all said the same thing, without me mentioning about the first person that suggested it. I then reached out to a place in town that would help me achieve my goals.

I would like to thank Amazon for publishing my book, Corinne L. Casazza for helping me gather my thoughts and focus my book into the right direction, my husband Chris who stood by my side, Diane from SCORE who got me started into this endeavor and everyone that has been a huge part of this great adventure.

Be well,

Samantha Conwell, October 25th, 2018

Chapter One

Surviving the NICU

It all started one cool crisp day; I started driving into the city to see one of the most terrifying places that I'd ever see. I scheduled to visit this place in December, right before Christmas, so the temperature outside was very cold but not snowing yet. I entered the street that I usually take to the hospital. My heart started racing. I couldn't grasp my breath. As I pulled into the parking deck, it seemed to be fuller than usual. I had to park on the 4th floor and take the elevator down. The elevator smelt like car oil and must.

I had on a sweatshirt, maternity pants and brown boots; my hair was pulled back so the wind wouldn't blow it around. As the elevator doors opened to leave the parking garage, a gust of wind came flying in. It made me feel like the walk was going to be much longer than it actually was. Once I reached the NICU department,

I rang the bell to let them know I was there. “Hello, how can I help you,” the receptionist answered. “Hi, I am here for my scheduled appointment with the provider, to discuss my son being placed into the NICU when he is born,” I said.

“Please wait, you’re early and the provider is not ready,” she replied.

I knew I was really early, but I’m always early. I was super nervous and my heart was beating fast, because they told me it would be about a half hour wait or so. I paced the hallway back and forth talking to my friend. “Let’s talk about something else, while we wait,” my friend said. We talked about the world and so much more, it felt like I knew her for much longer than I did, then the provider came and got us to come inside with him. We walked back into the lunchroom, where we were going to have our meeting with the doctor and my case manager nurse.

The doctor had kind eyes, and seemed to be intrigued with my son's case. "Why are you here? I've read your file, but would like to know in your own words why you are taking a tour."

"Well, we know my son will be transported to the NICU but we're still unsure why we need to put him in the NICU and what will take place while he is here," my voice trembled. I continued, "Because of the brain abnormalities, we're unsure what our son will need for resources."

"I'm very optimistic about your son's case and have a feeling he will do great," the provider responded. During this visit the provider asked me a bunch of questions, some of them were so hard to hear.

"Do you want us to resuscitate him? If need be. I don't think this will happen, but I have to ask," the provider explained.

When I went to answer him, I grabbed the top of my boots and was holding back tears. "Yes, I want you to take care of my son to the best of your abilities."

"Let's show you a room so you know what to expect," the provider said as he showed me an empty room.

"Why do you have so many refrigerators in here?" I was overwhelmed with all of the equipment in the room. I could feel my knees starting to shake.

"Because each one is for specific uses. One is for biohazards, another is for parents to keep drinks and food, the other one is for medicine that needs to be cold," the provider continued to explain. Meanwhile, I reminded myself that it would be another three months before he was here, and that I had to prepare myself for my tiny newborn son to arrive. It made me want to cry. I wished he could just be here now, so we could find out what was going on. But at the same time, I didn't want him to have a longer stay than he already had to have. I knew I wasn't going to be coming home with him, not for at least a few days after I was discharged. I kept to myself for the most part that he would have to go to the NICU, but I did tell a few people that I could rely on. The vision of the NICU room would haunt my dreams for the next few months.

On March 20th, 2018, my son was born, happy and ready for the world. The NICU nurses quickly did their job and took him away from me. They checked to make sure that he was fine and then they transported him down to the NICU. I only got to spend a few minutes with him, but they were the best few minutes. I told my husband that he could leave my side and go with our son, to make sure that they did everything that needed to be done. Luke's birth was planned via C-section. It was a repeat C-section, because I had a C-section for Zoey. I lay on the operating table worried, thinking that if something happened to him, I wouldn't see him because of my operation. How will I know if something happened? I didn't have a phone and couldn't reach my husband. As they finished fixing me up, they wheeled me down to my son's room in the NICU where my husband and friend were waiting.

Luke was in the bed, and I had to wait for the nurse to give me him, because he had wires everywhere. Luke was born at 8 pounds 1 ounce, so he wasn't as tiny as we were planning. When I saw him it was devastating and the nurse walked next to me while she went to grab my son. I started tearing up with fear because he looked so small, so fragile, and like he already went through so much. My friend took a photo of Luke and I, which I am very thankful for. But being in surgery for a couple of hours really tires you out, so I gave him to my husband and said, "I'll be right back." Then the nurse wheeled me to my room upstairs.

My mind was racing. I just wanted to be with my son, but then I would go back to thinking how much I missed my daughter and how I wanted to be with her. I called and texted the ones that needed to know he was here and when we could expect visitors. I also uploaded a photo to Facebook to let everyone that he arrived and to text or call us to check if it was okay to come see him.

Later that day in my son's room, I looked out at the city's skyline and prayed to be left alone with just my husband and son. My daughter was not allowed to come into the NICU because it was Flu season and the hospital has a strict policy on children visiting this department.

The pain in my heart was deep: something that can't be repaired by an empty conversation springing from false concern. I'd only told a handful of people when I was pregnant with him what was going on. Those people I trusted to care for our situation.

Being a mother going through this isn't easy, and knowing that there were only a few people that were actually truly concerned about my son, my daughter, my husband and I (the four of us, not just picking and choosing) was really sad. We wanted people there and we wanted to be happy, but I didn't want to answer anyone's questions.

The NICU changed me. Once I was so full of life and now I took everything so seriously. I hoped one day that I could become full of life again. The NICU makes you stronger. It makes you understand the pressures of what you expect from people and the outcomes you desire. I have come a long way from the NICU and I learned a lot along the way.

While Luke was in the NICU, he received a donated knitted hat that a group of individuals have made for the NICU, so they don't have to wear the standard pink/blue hats. His dark green hat was made from thick yarn and only fit him for a few days because his head circumference was too large for it. Still, I was thankful for this kind gesture.

There were a ton of students, nurses, doctors, and clinicians that would come in to visit my son. However, I only heard about a quarter of the visits.

"Hi, my name is Dr. Sage. I have some students with me and I'm part of your son's Neurology team. Could we come in?"

Dr. Sage spoke to her students and me about the ultrasound that was done. "Everything looks much better than what we were expecting, and he hasn't presented seizure like activity, so he doesn't an EEG. We'll still want to order an MRI to confirm the folds."

I knew there were other children that needed more help than my son, but I felt strongly that every visitor should be documented. That way, parents can follow up with any questions regarding their child's care.

Luke was only in the NICU for twenty-seven and a half hours, which may not seem like a lot, but it was hard. Every single second passed slowly. When he was discharged from the NICU, I took a photo of him and I. This way he could come join me in my room, with no other testing needed besides the MRI that was pending on the appointment. Or so we thought.

The NICU nurses sometimes made me feel like we weren't welcome: like his situation wasn't that bad. Or at least, that is how I perceived their body language. They were only in his room occasionally, and most of the time I had to ask for someone to come in. Everyone told me I'd get comfortable with the nurses and that they were kind, but I didn't feel that. Maybe it was because we were only there for a day and a few hours, but I expected a lot more. I kept repeating the things that I heard from others: that since he isn't a "preemie" he shouldn't be in the NICU. I just wanted to say to them, "If someone is in the ICU and doesn't die, then would you say that they shouldn't be there then?" I wondered why people would be so cruel and devastating.

I belong to some NICU groups, and I still haven't been able to share with them how long my son stayed in there because of the rude comments that others have endured. "Yes, I had a full-term baby, and yes we had a short stay." Mothers should realize everyone has their own journey, and not to judge others because their experience is different. Everyone that touches those NICU doors should realize that there are people that never get to hold their babies. Everyone is subject to their own destination, and it's hard enough to get there on your own without negative people.

We were still in close contact with the NICU. I knew we needed to schedule an MRI for Luke. "When will this MRI be done? I need to go home and be with my family. My daughter needs me," I said to my nurse.

"I called down to Radiology. He's on the list to be scanned but when an emergency comes in, then we have to take them before your son," the nurse replied.

I wanted to scream. I wanted to tell her, "He was just born, it's not like we could schedule this before hand. But there are enough machines in this place to do an MRI on him."

Finally, on Friday, he was taken away to have his MRI done. This was scary because they took off his medical bracelet (security), and wheeled him down while refusing to let me join him. I sat in my room worried because yet again he wasn't with me. A couple of hours later he came back and I was so relieved that we were together again.

Soon after we'd be on our way to our home and getting settled in with both kids. This was going to be the best adventure in our lives. Or so we thought.

Chapter Two

Building a Family from Two to Three to Four

It all started with the two of us. I can't even imagine just the two of us. My husband and I met at my former place of work, Applebee's. I was a host while putting myself through college. I met my husband on a Thursday night. He was out with a few of my old classmates for their typical guys night. I saw one of my friends and leaned over. "Hey, who's your friend over there? The one with the straight teeth and nice hair?"

My friend laughed. "Oh Sam. I can give him your number if you want." That's how it began. I had just turned 21 and he was 22.

Our first and second date was for the books. We'd always remember those nights -- crystal clear. We made plans over the phone to meet at T.G.I. Friday's in Methuen, MA at 7 pm on January 6th, 2009. There was a lot of snow on the ground that evening and we were about to get another storm. I arrived early as usual. Even in bad weather I loved to be early because I hated being late. Chris arrived shortly after our agreed time to meet. “Sorry I’m late,” Chris said with a smirk. “I was at the gym.”

I smiled. “That’s okay, I need to start going to the gym.”

“Yeah, you do,” he laughed.

I immediately texted my friend and told him that he owed me big time and drinks were going to be on him, LOL. I was a little insulted, and thought “who is this kid?” He is really bold. Here I was 115 pounds and 5 feet tall, so I was on the petite side. We had a great first date; we got to know each other and had a lot of laughs. The second date night -- will just have to wait for another time.

We were inseparable. A few years later, we got an apartment together. “What a relief,” I said. It was about time we start a future and grow together.

“What shall we do next?” Chris asked.

“Well, we can start going on more adventures,” I quickly replied.

We spent years traveling: going snowboarding up north, traveled to Florida, Wales, London, Connecticut, New York and Canada. We spent almost a decade doing this. The year prior to Chris proposing, we went to Wales and London with our friends. Wow, it was so amazing! I fell in love with Wales and the family we stayed with.

On, October 25th, 2014, Chris proposed and it was so amazing. He took me to the movies near Boston Common where we saw Alexander and the Terrible, Horrible, Not Good, Very Bad Day with Steve Carell. It was really funny. Chris took me for a walk and we bumped into my dad and uncle. We started dancing in the middle of the gazebo in the Common. My dad and uncle began taking photos. I could hear Chris’s heart beating fast. His breathing became labored and I could tell something was going to happen. Chris got down on one knee and asked, “Samantha, will you marry me?”

I waited a few seconds but my husband will tell you it felt a lot longer than that. “YES!” I replied.

We began calling everyone that was close to us with so much excitement. I was so blessed that my family was there to be part of this special moment. Then all of the wedding planning began. After a little less than a year of planning, we got married on October 9th, 2015. However, on September 18th, 2015, I found out that I was pregnant with our first child.

On that day, I woke up early to go to work and thought to myself, “Hhhhmmm, I feel weird. I think it’s that time of the month, but I’ll just double check.” I took a pregnancy test. As I hovered over the stick, I thought that if it came back positive, then I’d at least be grateful we weren’t getting married in a church. As I watched the stick go from one line to two, my heart melted: I was so excited and couldn’t wait to tell Chris. Chris was still sleeping, so I went to work without telling him. I figured I would plan something. That day my future husband was extra talkative. He would just send me random texts saying, "hi," and "I love you," while I was dying at my desk because I didn't want to say a word. When I got out of work, I rushed to the grocery store. I got a cake and had the baker write, "Thanks for knocking me up." Soon, Chris got home from work and I videotaped the whole thing. I had bought a couple of onesies and Chris was so overwhelmed with joy!

We were finishing planning our wedding and honeymoon and now, we were beginning to plan for a baby as well. We went on our honeymoon to the incredible Aruba, where the scenery and people we encountered were amazing. We had an all-inclusive resort, which was great despite not being able to drink. I had a ton of food instead, though I probably had more than I expected LOL.

When we got home, there was so much planning and renovations that we had to go through in our apartment. On

January 6th, 2016, which was our 7th dating anniversary, we found out that we were having a girl! It was very exciting news! We announced the gender at our reveal party; at you guessed it, T.G.I. Friday's. We had planned for a dinner where everyone could eat and have a good time. The whole restaurant was cheering with excitement for us.

We had our daughter on May 29th, 2016, after one full week past my due date. I went through 31 hours of labor and an emergency C-section. I delivered my daughter at a New England Hospital. It was an incredible journey, which no one knew would prepare me for one of my greatest journeys in recovery years later.

That first year of Zoey's life and being a mom was fantastic. It had its moments though. There were times at home that I felt like something or someone was missing. I couldn't help but look at my daughter and say, "You need a best friend for life: someone that will always stand by your side and help you through hard moments. A person who won't judge you because you make a mistake and won't gang up on you because you have your own voice. Someone who can stand next to you and defend your choice."

Right before my daughter's first birthday, I went off birth control and we started trying to conceive again. We didn't tell many people. In fact, we only mentioned it to my sister and the Godparents because we knew they would be excited for us.

Shortly after my daughter's birthday, I took a pregnancy test on July 13th, 2017 at 5:24 am. I hovered over the test for three minutes praying it would come back positive and it did. I watched the stick go from one line to two. It said I was pregnant! I was so very excited and couldn't wait to tell Chris that we were having another baby! Once again, this was first thing in the morning. So I said to my husband, "have a great day! Zoey and I will see you when you get home. Maybe we could do lunch."

I told Zoey, but she didn't understand the concept fully at this point because she was only thirteen months. I still had such a fun day with Zoey. I used the phone to call around places, to see if I could find somewhere that had a "Promoted to Big Sister Shirt." I called all over the place: the Rockingham Mall, Buy Buy Baby, Target, etc. I remembered that we were close to Baby's R Us so I called them and they only had one left. I had them put it on hold and my daughter and I went to Salem, NH to grab it. We went to customer service when we arrived and I was frantic. I was pressed for time and needed to get things done. "Hi, I'm the one that called for the last "Promoted to Big Sister" long sleeve shirt!"

"Sure ma'am. Right this way. I have placed it in the back so we wouldn't sell it before you got here," the customer service lady said.

"THANK YOU! THANK YOU! THANK YOU! You have no idea how excited I am! You made my day," I was screaming with excitement!

I was so pumped that we rushed home, I cleaned up the house, and I texted Chris asking him to come home for lunch. He didn't know I couldn't wait to tell him. I set up on my phone to record my husband coming in the room.

"Hey, do you like the new shirt I got Zoey?"

My husband looked at it and then said, "Promoted to Big, Sister?! WHAT!! Okay!" He was so excited and then later on that night, he told me he couldn't really work because he was so distracted by the news.

We started telling a few people that weekend, as well as throughout the first trimester. I wanted to wait until after my 30th birthday to tell everyone else that was not in touch with us: like our Facebook friends or extended relatives. After the first trimester, we announced to everyone that we were having another baby. I set up four plush sharks in a row, because everyone who knows me knows I love sharks! I wrote a card for each one of them and it said, "Dadda Shark, Momma Shark, Zoey Shark, and Coming Soon Shark." People went nuts about the announcement: they all thought it was great and that it suited us so well. We had so much love and support and everyone was overjoyed. I started doing my monthly appointments with my doctor, which was going very well, and I didn't even have morning sickness, which was a plus!

My husband and I thought it would be difficult taking my daughter with me to my appointments. We also wanted her to play with kids her own age and not just older kids, so we decided to put her in daycare. She was only 16 months old and I still remember the way I felt. I cried when we dropped her off, then proceeded to sob all day until my eyes were red and swollen. To this day, even though I know she's fine and that daycare is good for her, I still cry. I still want her to be the little girl that would look at me without hurt. In my mind, I let Zoey down by bringing her to daycare during a critical time in her development. I blame myself every day but this is something I have to live with. Other moms may have a different perspective, but this killed me. I would stay in the driveway at daycare: bawling so hard because I felt like I was failing her. I knew that she was crying when I left, but every time I would text the provider she would let me know that she didn't cry for long. It still hurt, and I had no idea what was lurking around the corner.

Chapter Three

The Worries and Unnecessary Stressors

My stressors increased throughout my pregnancy because the larger I got, the harder it was to move around. Then I worried more and more about my daughter and how she was doing. I did have people who actually cared about me help my family get through these obstacles.

In the beginning when we first found out, I couldn't even look at my husband without feeling devastated: thinking to myself why do these things happen? Why can't I fix it? It would be months before my husband and I could have a regular date night without talking about it. But time has proven that my husband has been great through this entire experience and he has provided for us every step of the way. He let me make decisions: sometimes the wrong ones but he still stood by my side. Sometimes people make a wrong decision and it just depends on how you deal with it. It tells people about your character.

There have been so many sources that have made this journey easy or hard. Many people have reached out to me during this time. However, there were more people that didn't. Some people talked badly about me: whether they were judging me from reading a Facebook post or badgering about my GoFundMe page to raise money for a service dog. I also had groups shame me and other moms like me. It could happen because I didn't breastfeed either child, or because my son wasn't in the NICU for the same (or longer) time than their babies. People also felt strongly that because my son wasn't a preemie, he didn't belong there at all. There is so much hate out there and it needs to stop. It can start with you! One day at a time.

When the GoFundMe Page started, I had put myself out there because of complications that had occurred with my back. I received a lot of negative comments, but I also received positive comments. Some people reached out and gave me great suggestions and advice. I raised a small amount of money and I'm still continuing to save for a service dog. However, the costs are unreal. It's not like getting a puppy: these dogs cost $10,000 or more and there is at least a two or three year waiting list. It was extremely stressful putting myself out there because people only saw a screenshot of what was going on and felt free to judge and try to shame me.

Some of the Facebook groups that I had belonged to were very judgmental and not kind at all. Before I posted anything on these group sites, I'd wait for someone in a similar situation to post and see what the responses were. I'm glad I did that because in one of the groups, this mom was chewed out because her baby was full-term in the NICU. The moms that had preemie babies tore this lady apart and I was glad it wasn't me. This made me very concerned, so I started a group on Facebook called the Full-Term Babies NICU Group. Now people have a safe place to voice their concerns and their stories.

I've had multiple groups say that I was an awful mom because I didn't breastfeed my children. What they don't know is that I couldn't. With both of my children my breasts were like rocks. They hurt so bad, and I was getting scabs all over my breast from my son latching. This was incredibly painful.

All the comments that I received, both good and bad, have made me a stronger person. They've given me clarity and understanding that there are some things you need to care about and others that you don't. Some people you need and others you need to just move on.

There was a point that I didn't want any communication with anyone, which is okay but it gets lonely when you do this. Not everyone respects boundaries and space, but you need to stand your ground and know that you don't need to share any information if you don't want to.

I started seeing a therapist for a separate issue before my daughter's first birthday. I was very lucky that I was seeing her because when I heard the news about my son, I needed to make sure the decisions I was making were the right ones for my family. My therapist let me know if something was a little extreme, or if it was just right.

Looking back, letting certain people in was the best thing in our lives, while letting others in was the worse idea. They were the people that told me things like, "you're thinking too much into it," or "doctors don't know what they are talking about." It drove me nuts to be told that I was "being a worrying hypochondriac," or that "technology is wrong all the time." These people made me second-guess every decision. These people aren't you, aren't going through your emotions, and certainly aren't respecting you. Do yourself a favor and limit what you tell these people because you need to listen to yourself and keep your own counsel. You are a rock and you need others that will build with you.

I will never apologize for having a difference of an opinion or a different path. I've been through so much, so many battles that I need to pick which war I want to win. The war of life, the war of love, the war of strength. When you are a young family without a tribe, it's hard to allow more people in. The number of people in your tribe is the product of what you are. Have those that bring you peace and strength, like the ocean. The ocean may be made up of water, and it's gorgeous when it's calm. But when it's fierce, it's more powerful than land.

Chapter Four

16 Weeks & Beyond

We brought our daughter Zoey to see the first ultrasound of her sibling. We thought she might enjoy seeing it. The tech asked us if we wanted to know the gender. I had thought about it for a minute because I knew we were having a gender reveal party that weekend. It was the sixteen-week appointment, we thought it was going to be a magical day but it turned out that God had bigger plans and ideas for us.

We found out we were having a boy and we were so very excited. I had my husband leave the room with my daughter because she was very curious and wanted to go into every drawer there. The tech said that the doctor would be in to do her sets of ultrasounds, which is totally normal. When the physician came in, she had a student with her, which is also normal because this is a teaching hospital. The physician starting asking me genetic questions. I didn't think anything of it until she asked me to call my husband back in the room so they could discuss the results.

My husband and I felt scared: Chris was sitting by my bedside with Zoey. As soon as the doctor started talking, I had my hands down on my lap and my heart started racing. I felt numb and didn't hear a thing the doctor was saying except that something was wrong. My instant thought was to get out of that room and go to my obstetrician now. I was screaming inside, I had to pull myself out of the daze and grab my daughter before she touched anything she was not supposed to. I looked over to see my husband who looked like he was going to pass out. Luckily, he was sitting in the chair and leaning back. I looked over to the doctor, and asked, "Can I stay in the room until Dr. MacKay is ready to see me, because I can't sit in the waiting room with all the smiling people?"

They agreed and brought me to a genetic counselor. I don't remember who she was or what she had to offer. I just looked her in the eyes and asked to leave. I just wanted to see my doctor and no one else, and I didn't want any more people looking at me or judging me.

We had the gender reveal party and all I wanted to do was scream, throw things, breakdown, and cry. I had to pick up the balloons that were waiting for me as well as grab some last-minute things. I was running late, which has only been one other time in my life (my wedding rehearsal). I was in such a panic because it was a Saturday on the 125 in Plaistow, NH: a place typically as busy as a parking lot.

We held a gender reveal party. With a gender reveal party, you don't need to know what the gender is: you can simply ask the technician not tell you. Then you have him or her write it down in an envelope so you can go to the party store or a bakery and give them the envelope so they can get your balloon order together.

People do gender reveal parties differently. We chose the method of balloons so our daughter could be a major part of it. As a side note, I'm glad I found out with my husband because when I went to pick up the balloon order at the party store, they didn't complete my order and had left the gender balloons out in the open.

"Are these yours?" The clerk asked with a puzzled look on her face.

"Yes, these are mine. Luckily I already know what I'm having. We ordered these three days ago." I was not amused.

Meanwhile, my husband was getting my daughter and himself ready. We had to be at the venue before our guests arrived and some people were going to arrive early. This is usually fine, but I was about 10 minutes late everywhere I went because it was a Saturday.

"Oh well, it's not like they can start without us," I explained to my husband. You could tell he was annoyed because he knew a few guests were going to arrive early.

I was so ashamed that I couldn't make it there before my guests. I was reserved during the party and tried my best not to withdraw. My sister told me my Grandmother was in the hospital. I was even more upset because I would've been there instead of this party!

I tried to stick to a few people for lengthy conversations: only those that I knew wouldn't ask too many questions or could talk about something other than the baby. I became nervous when it was time for the gender reveal. I didn't want to start screaming because in my mind I was already there. My palms began to sweat and I watched people as we opened the bag. Everyone (including us) cheered, but I only pretended to be excited on the outside. Inside, I felt empty and lost with the knowledge that my grandma was in the hospital and there was something wrong with my son.

I knew that no one was aware that this was going on, but I kept telling myself to keep my head high. I held my tongue and made sure that I was restricted from people touching me, because I didn't want to break down and cry. I feared that I would start telling everyone, but I didn't want anyone to look at me with a sad face or say "you poor thing."

The following week, I was back seeing my providers for additional testing. I had an appointment with my new primary care physician because my health insurance required it.

My PCP told me I had a mood disorder at the first appointment that we had together. He had only a screenshot of my life and it just happened to be the most devastating part of my life. (Bad timing to judge someone on their mood.) At this point, I had already been officially asked to terminate my pregnancy 10 times: not including the times I spoke to any provider on the phone. I honestly don't think a PCP should be able to write these diagnosis codes, especially if they only have met the patient once at a particularly difficult time in their life. Since then, I've requested that they remove this from my record. I've been to a therapist who confirmed that I don't have a mood disorder.

When looking through research, sometimes anxiety is listed under mood disorders, however it can qualify for other conditions. I have since left this provider and am doing much better at a different facility. Of course people have some anxiety about the unknown. If you don't, then you're not human.

With being asked 10 times to terminate my pregnancy, I felt upset and it got worse every time they asked. I had a lot of anger, which was perceived by others as me being rude or controlling. If they had any idea what I was going through, they might have opened their eyes.

I'm a pro-life type of person and also a Catholic. We don't believe in abortions, however I don't judge those that choose to have abortions. I just knew that this wasn't the path for us.

I knew my son would be okay, and that I would do everything to make sure that he was loved and cared for. But I didn't understand why I was constantly asked to end my pregnancy. It's okay for some people because of the unknown and the worry. For us, it was the total opposite. God gave us a miracle and he wanted to show me a new path in life. Every time they asked, I'd break down in tears. I'd weep into my hands while they told me it was okay and that they just wanted to give me options.

In one of the New England states like Massachusetts, the law states that you can terminate a pregnancy up to 24 weeks. I like to do research, so I researched late term abortions and what exactly they do during this procedure. It was very graphic and sometimes I still have nightmares about it.

Since I could feel my son move at 16-weeks, I couldn't bear doing this to a baby. I just wanted to tell them to stop asking me because it felt like peer pressure. If they'd just hand out brochures to patients and have them meet with either a social worker or a therapist to confirm their choice, then they should be fine. If they're worried about the hospital being sued, have the patient sign a waiver. If people have all the accurate information and the proper resources, they could make an accurate decision for themselves. Once this decision is made, it should be mandatory that the provider can't ask again. This is how #StopAsking became my savior! This hashtag, I am hoping will help those that want to continue with their pregnancy and would like to stop being asked about this. Hospitals need to design a better outlet for moms because these decisions are not meant to taken lightly.

Chapter Five

Doctors, Nurses, and Ongoing Appointments

With the ongoing appointments, they ranged from normal OB visits to M.R.I.'s. I had twelve appointments before Christmas. These included regular appointments, genetic appointments, a fetal echocardiogram, neurology appointments, high risk pregnancy consultations, M.R.I.'s, Neurosurgeon visits, and the NICU tour. I dreaded these appointments because I didn't want to be harassed about terminating my pregnancy.

After the New Year, I had another twelve appointments prior to my delivery day: from ultrasounds to traditional appointments. With all these hospital visits, I'd missed a lot of my daughter's life because I had to put her in daycare: something which made me sad. I was sad because I was giving my daughter a sibling, a best friend for life, but I was missing time with her and she was learning to live without me.

These countless tests were not limited to those 24 weeks. I also had a lot of blood work that was required. The phone calls consisted of providers calling me and me calling them for testing results. For my M.R.I. results, I could get the information directly after the appointments.

I spent most of my time at the hospital of my choosing and not once was I referred to a designated children's hospital. This children's hospital is much more equipped for the pediatric scene than the hospital that I attend. Don't get me wrong, the hospital that I attend still has a great pediatric department. However, when they admitted that they'd never seen this combination before, they should have referred us to a better facility. I felt like the doctors and case managers didn't have my son's best interests in mind. I felt alone, scared, and I put my trust in those people that needed to give me all the opinions.

After my son was born, we had a few appointments: ultrasounds, M.R.I.'s and other testing. Even though we didn't want my son to have surgery, we'd been told that they'd discuss surgery if his cyst kept increasing.

My son had a combination of an interhemispheric cyst, agenesis of the corpus callosum, and polymicrogyria. In the next chapter I will discuss what all of these mean. The interhemispheric cyst was the first thing that was presented in my son's ultrasound at 16 weeks, and the rest followed.

I became so frightened that I felt like I was never being understood. It seemed like they never heard me and that I wasn't getting the education I needed to make the best decisions for my son or our family. I asked around and found a doctor at a children's hospital where we found my son's neurosurgeon. To this day October 9th, 2018 my son has not had a seizure and hasn't needed surgery!!!

There were lots of providers that made a difference and were a part of both mine and my son's care. Dr. MacKay is very intelligent and super nice. She has been my OB/GYN and has been so for years because she has both a positive and amazing spirit. When I was brought to see her after receiving the hard news, she let me speak before giving me options. She's really great with her bedside manner towards her patients. Throughout my pregnancy, Dr. MacKay always kept in touch with me to make sure that everything is all right.

"So, how did this past M.R.I. go? Have there been any changes?"

"The cyst has enlarged but remains inside of the proportions where we won't need to have surgery," I replied.

She would make sure I had the resources I needed. We agreed that we'd schedule a C-section prior to my 40 week due date because of the situation that was unfolding.

Dr. MacKay agreed with my decision to keep my baby and stated that a C-section would be the safer option for both of us. She took a picture before and after the C-section with me. She even visited me on the postpartum floor while my son and I were there. She's truly one of the only doctors that holds a special place in my heart.

Caroline is one of Dr. MacKay's nurses and she is an awesome RN! She has been with me through both pregnancies. She cheered me on while I was attending school and let me cry in her arms every time I saw her. She praised me when I was having a good day and helped me get through the rough ones. She always tried to make me feel comfortable at every appointment: even if she was giving me a tetanus shot. (Remember Caroline, how I tried to talk my way out of it?). She made me feel secure in being sad, happy, or whatever else I was feeling. She didn't perceive me like I was a sad person: just a person who was dealt something that they were trying to overcome. She helped me record my sons' heartbeat on the Doppler. She made me feel safe and even stopped by to see my son and me on a postpartum floor.

One of the nurses that had helped me and my family through all of this was Faith P., and she was so amazing. She would answer all of my questions even if it was at eleven o'clock night. She took the time to call me the same day that I found out about Luke's brain malformation. She had scheduled an M.R.I. for me two days later, and she told us that she'd meet us there. She did, and I asked her a bunch of questions after I got dressed into the required scrubs. I laid in the M.R.I. machine while they brought my husband in so he could sit at the head of the bed. I was freezing once the M.R.I. started, so they wrapped me in a warm blanket.

Faith would check in on me and I'd keep in touch with her. She went to see my son after he was born in the NICU and she still checks up on my son regularly. I'll even email photos to her.

During my delivery with Zoey, the anesthesiology team and department were amazing and perfect! I felt safe, and the staff was on point with every single thing that they were doing. During my son's delivery, this was a whole different story.

These providers and healthcare professionals have really changed me for the best and have helped me focus on what was truly needed. Some of these providers have changed me and encouraged me not to trust certain people and to rely on others. With every person I met, and with every journey I took throughout this time, each provider held a certain place.

Chapter Six

Diagnosis from Interhemispheric Cyst to Agenesis Corpus Callosum

Some of my son's diagnoses were complex cerebral malformation, left frontal polymicrogyria, callosal agenesis, massa intermedia, and interhemispheric cysts. These results occurred at the 16 weeks appointment and most of them have been determined within the last few months. Some of these diagnoses are hard to hear because it has been so long since we found out about the small cyst that was developing in his brain. There's still so much of it that's unknown though, like how he'll respond to the development. As a precaution, we've been doing physical therapy since my son was three months old.

It's a good thing I'm a mother who loves doing research to figure out why this happened. I wanted to know what I could do moving forward, so I began looking into .org websites. I looked at these websites because there was a doctor that I worked for who recommended the .org websites for their more trustworthy information as opposed to .com ones. This way I knew the information I was looking at was accurate.

I said to myself, "my son is perfect. He is a happy baby and is acting exactly like he should be." Some things he's still working on, but he's doing such a great job meeting his milestones when he can. Speaking from my experience as a mom, it can be very difficult when you have to show up to every appointment only to feel increasingly bombarded by new information. Sometimes it's okay to take a breather from the late night research and worrying so you can just enjoy the kids that are right in front of you.

We knew about the interhemispheric cyst way before our son was born, and the callosal agenesis was already known. By the time my son was four months old, he had already been through three M.R.I.'s but luckily only the minimum amount of blood work. The more times we went to the doctor, the longer the diagnoses became. The one thing I loved about switching to the children's hospital is they were more understanding with his diagnoses, but they made sure that they stood up for the patient. Countless times we heard, "well Luke isn't showing signs that we need to do anything extensive at this time." This was always great news to hear, and I was so very thankful to hear that.

Struggling with these diagnoses, there were no groups around my area that could help me in the way that I needed. Each one of these diagnoses was unique in their own aspect but at the same token: not combined in any group. I also couldn't speak about it in the NICU mom groups because I just felt like someone was going to shame me .

There is no one disorder that combined the diagnoses of the interhemispheric cyst, agenesis corpus callosum, and pmg, a.k.a. polymicrogyria. If we had the right group, the right source, or the right comfort, it would've been an easier thing to endure. Each one of these findings can be devastating and cause a lot of growth for the person going through those changes.

I've learned a lot by switching to the children's hospital. The providers explained to me in depth what each of the diagnoses are and I would love to share it with you.

Polymicrogyria is an abnormal development prior to birth where the fetus has too many folds in the brain. It seems like the common case that continues to appear in all of my research is that this is caused by some sort of infection during pregnancy; another possible cause is genetic mutation. (U.S. National Library of Medicine). After delivering my daughter, I had a huge infection that caused green fluid to leak everywhere. These include but are not limited to green mucus from my nose, green vomit, green urine, and so forth. My incision burn as it leaked green pus and this pain coupled with a severe abdominal discomfort. It was quite a show. I felt lost and helpless that we never figured out what it was or the cause's true identity.

This was ongoing until my daughter was ten months old and I went through a bunch of testing that ultimately never found the cause. Fast forward to when I was pregnant with my son and I had a UTI. The provider prescribed me Macrobid, which took care of the infection. I can't help but think that the infection that I had after delivering my daughter carried through into my next pregnancy, even though it was four months after my infection disappeared.

During my pregnancy with my son, we had only discovered a few things: the diagnoses of the interhemispheric cyst, agenesis of the corpus callosum, and the pmg. There have been other findings in the diagnoses that have us on a progressive track to move forward in benefitting him and his quality of life. My son is six months old and doing fantastic. We saw a feeding specialist to help him with eating (so far we only saw them once) and we do physical therapy, but he's doing great. For every milestone he makes, whether it be the "normal" baby schedule or his own, we take in the milestones that he does.

We only used the feeding specialist once! This is such a great thing! He also just put weight on his feet to stand on the floor and he is starting to roll.

I looked all over the city and found no groups that supported my needs, so I decided to reach out to places that had these types of groups. It helped me come up with an idea. I've always wanted to make a huge difference in people's lives and telling my story about my son and my family is one of the stepping stones.

Callosal agenesis is the lack of the corpus callosum and is very common in a lot of people. Most people don't even know that they're missing it and they have no deficits. But on the other hand, they may not possess other diagnoses like Luke's to set them back. The intricate details that go into the brain are remarkable: especially with the brain's ability to adapt. The younger you are, the greater the chances are that your brain will correct itself. Sometimes this is not the case, but sometimes it is. We just have to believe that everything happens for a reason and we're here to know more about life than just what we want. My son has taught me so much about being grateful about life.

An Interhemispheric Cyst that my son has is a fluid sac, which starts from the frontal lobe and extends to the third ventricle of his brain. The cyst has two compartments but the fluid doesn't have any blood, tumor, or cancer within the sac. This is such great news that any parent can hear!

Chapter Seven

Research about birthing help

Everyone needs help sometimes. The research and the families I've met along the way have truly helped me. I reached out privately to many people and organizations.

My suggestion is that if you don't want to share your story with your family and friends, do so with a group. This doesn't mean you have to drive to a group every week; we all know the amount of appointments that are needed.

Find a group online through Facebook, Twitter, or Instagram. If you can't do that, you can even contact your local community action facility. Those people are here for you. They'll try to meet your needs in every way. Some PCPs have case managers that will come to your home for visits, and this is very beneficial.

Make sure you find a suitable Home Health Visiting Nurse, because you should be provided one when you go home: at least for one check. From what I learned, this usually applies to those who have had a C-section.

Depending on your health insurance, they should cover the visiting nurse at full cost. But call and check with them or ask your case manager to provide this for you. Some insurance companies will reimburse you for the purchase of a car seat; they should reimburse you for taking a birth class. I would recommend a birth class, but go there with an open mind: don't just assume that you'll be having a natural vaginal birth like I did. Ask a lot of questions. That's why you're there.

Ask for assistance for financial support if your income allows it. Request parking vouchers if you're at the hospital more frequently than not for additional procedures and testing. If they can't provide you with parking passes, ask if they have an extra discounted rate for patients on a certain budget (you may need to provide tax information though).

Also, having a Doula is a great benefit. A Doula is very beneficial before the birth and even after. Some Doulas will run errands and help with house cleaning. But sometimes it's a pricier option depending on their experience and what they offer.

You could have a live-at-home or a visiting nanny. There are multiple resources out there: you just have to continue to ask providers, social workers, case managers, friends, families, or even just good old Google. There are even agencies dedicated to helping you find a live-in nanny.

These nannies come from another country, and there are some requirements that you have to follow. Not only will you have an interview, background, and criminal check, but you'll also have a house check to make sure they aren't living like "Cinderella." The agency requires you to have the following to become part of this organization: you must dish out $10,000 a year for a membership. You must pay the nanny $200 a week plus one college course while she works for you, provide two weeks paid time off, room and board, as well as a car so she can enjoy her time off. They are also strict about how much the person can technically work.

The agency doesn't allow nannies to work any more than 45 hours a week, and a schedule has to be given to the person prior to their arrival so he or she can plan for their activities. This would be a great option for a surgeon or a doctor because they have the financial resources, and sometimes depending on the employer, they may reimburse you.

Sometimes couples, moms, and dads DO NOT have a village of people to help raise their kids. A lot of times, it's not because they choose this option, it's just how it happened to be. You have to really trust someone and know they'll follow the rules when you allow them to help you. Some moms and dads believe that only certain people should be a part of the healthy development of your child or children.

Having different resources for nannies, daycares, babysitters, doulas and much more will help keep the stress down on the family that are going through hardships.

Chapter Eight

Delivery

WOW! There were many negative experiences in my son's delivery, but there were some pretty cool moments too. My husband and I walked to the hospital from the condo we rented with my parents so they could stay with our daughter.

"Bye Zoey. I'll miss you and I love you very much. Mommy is going to the hospital for awhile."

It was the first day of Spring. I began to cry while we were walking out the door because I knew how much I was going to miss Zoey. At this point, she was my whole world.

The day was freezing. My husband checked the temperature and it said twenty-three degrees out (pretty chilly). We made it to the hospital, checked in at 8:00am, and I was taken back with a nurse shortly after. I didn't feel any connection with this nurse.

She was semi-friendly but not enough to make me feel comfortable about having a baby and to be in her care. She seemed to treat me like I was only a number and that this was not a very exciting time.

She got me set up with everything I needed. Shortly afterwards, an anesthesiologist came into my room.

"Hi, I'm Dr. Soverign. I'll be doing your epidural and spinal block today. I have a consent form that I need to go over with you and have you sign."

"Okay, but I'm super nervous and don't want anything to go wrong. I have a daughter at home and need everything to go smooth."

"Don't worry, we do this all the time and nothing will happen."

I tried to shake my nervousness. While I laid in the hospital bed, I stayed quiet: not mentioning anything to my husband about how worried I was. I told him, "everything would be fine and I'll see you in there."

My obstetrician came in, we got a before picture together (I just love her, in a professional way! She is so sweet), and she explained to me some of the particulars. This include who exactly would be in the room, the options of a clear screen or a blue screen, and roughly how long the C-section procedure was going to take. She gave me a big hug and told me that she would meet me in there.

The anesthesiologist's body language made me uncomfortable from the beginning. I found out she was a student: not an attending physician. I learned this after she made an injection into my back: misplacing the epidural in the wrong cavity before telling her superior that she missed.

"It's in the wrong spot."

"That's okay, just take it out and re-adjust it."

I wanted to scream, but I couldn't from the way I was positioned. I was hunched over and the nurse who brought me in was holding me in the somewhat fetal position on the side of the operating table. I couldn't breathe. I wanted to start panicking but I didn't have anyone in the operating room that I knew. No one to save me. No one to speak for me. I don't know how many attempts she made because they injected me with the lidocaine so I couldn't feel anything. But when she placed the epidural into the wrong cavity, you bet your bottom I almost flew off the table! My whole right side was killing me and it felt like I got an electric shock.

Of course, this happened all before Dr. MacKay was present. This would be one of the toughest journeys of my life. Later I'd discover there's only one other case study like mine and that one was self-inflicted: not medically induced by a medical professional.

I wished I knew she was a student, because I would have never allowed her do it. I couldn't find her name on my record (at least the one they gave me) to report her. My life would become harder and harder, soon after.

I truly wished my doctor was in there with me. I'm not sure if she would say something, but it would have given me comfort knowing that someone who knew my whole journey was there.

After the epidural was placed (finally), they had to put in a catheter. This requires you to be fully exposed on the operating table.

There was a woman at my feet on my left side. I had no idea who she was, or why she was there. While the nurse was placing the catheter, she was staring at my genitals and that made me very uncomfortable and disgusted. I wanted to say, "What are you staring at? Don't you have a job to do? Why don't you go do it? You're disgusting just sitting there staring. You have no part of this. Go do your shit and give me some privacy." But of course, I didn't say anything.

About 30 minutes in or so, my husband was allowed to come in and wait with me. My husband already had the video camera (GoPro). We waited patiently while the doctor informed the staff to change the curtain to clear so I could see my son when he was born. He was so handsome!

Luke was born at 10:55 am, and hearing him crying was the best moment of my life besides hearing my daughter cry for the first time. I started crying when I saw him, and then the nurses took him away.

While my husband and I were looking at our son through the curtain, a nurse came over and told us that we needed to stop recording. She demanded this directly after Luke was born.

"Stop recording. You can't be recording now."

"Okay. Sam I have to shut off the camera."

"NO!"

"Sir, you have to stop recording."

"STOP RECORDING? LIKE WHAT THE FUCK LADY?!" This was our sons' birth. Granted, I believe that this nurse was part of the NICU. However, who gives a shit if she is? This is my son's birth. We knew he was going to be fine. We just saw him moving on the ultrasound and we weren't having a vaginal delivery. He was already out: he was fine and he cried.

If there were any problems, we would have seen it on the ultrasound: especially since we took one right before delivery. This girl didn't know two licks about me. She had no idea about the testing I went through, and you'll soon find out why I have said this about the NICU nurses. (They were supposed to be my rock, or at least that was what I was led to believe).

I was told prior that there might be a chance that my son might be a stillborn, but that still wouldn't have stopped me from capturing his birth! I wish my husband didn't agree with this nurse. She had no right saying that, and I am shocked that no one in the operating room pulled her aside and told her to stop. I want patients to stand up to these people. It's your day with your baby and nothing should stop you from capturing a moment. Good or bad, you have prepared yourself for the moment for so long.

Shortly after this, my husband went down with my son to the NICU. Before I left the operating room, I was able to get a quick picture with Dr. MacKay! I shortly was moved back to a labor and delivery room to recover from my surgery.

Once I was stabilized we took the elevator down to the NICU. As I was lying on the stretcher, I was super nervous to see my son. I was rolled in and saw my husband with Luke and one of our best friends there keeping my husband company (as he did with Zoey's birth). I was able to hold Luke for a few minutes before they had to wheel me to my room, where I was going to finish recovering.

Holding my son in the NICU was bittersweet. I remember his soft skin and his handsome face. I was so sad. I didn't want to leave him but at the same time, I was exhausted from surgery.

We had some visitors, which was overwhelming this time around. Everyone of course wanted to see Luke, but I was separated from him for quite some time. I let people hold him, and there were moments that I wanted everyone to leave. But I told myself it was okay to feel like shit. I just had a major procedure and a baby! I knew I was okay to have mixed feelings while this day was progressing. To have to see your child in the NICU is surreal and nothing can prepare you for it.

My sister and my husband brought me back upstairs which was really nice because I got to spend some time with my sister. But soon her and my husband would have to leave, and it would just be me: alone in a double bedroom.

Soon after, I was determined to go see my son. So after twelve hours of being in the operating room, I was finally down in the NICU: reunited with my son. I got to spend some moments alone with Luke and enjoy him without any interruptions. It was amazing, but I was sad at the same time. While everyone was gone (which was nice), I was so sad that Zoey wasn't there. She was with my parents and all I wanted was to see her. I felt like I abandoned her and I began to cry.

The next day was hard. I went to the NICU, where I spent a few hours with my son and providers. However, I wanted to take my son out and bring him upstairs with me. It was March 21st, 2018 at 2:05 pm when I finally brought my son upstairs to a regular room and he was busting out of the NICU for good. This was a lot sooner than we were originally planning!

My progression throughout the next day was going great until late that night. That's when I began to have a headache and was dizzy to where I couldn't stand or it would feel like I was going to pass out. After speaking to the nurse about this, she informed the anesthesiology team right away. They spent some time with me: going over my symptoms and which procedures I had. They gave me the options of a pain patch or a blood patch.

I have seen so many good people go down the wrong path, even from just the first time of using a pain patch. I was not going to be another statistic! I wanted to try another way: a way that seemed simple at the time. It seemed like the quicker solution, but it turned out it wasn't.

During this time, it was only Luke and I in the room; I didn't have Chris in the room because he was with Zoey and my parents at the condo. During this time, I looked up the blood patch online to see if I could find anything on this topic. I did, but I had to take care of Luke, so I wasn't too focused on what I was reading. Sometimes I regret getting the blood patch done because I feel like even though we discussed the risks, I felt like I didn't know much information on the topic.

Having the blood patch was the worst experience of my life, including child labor and delivery. They brought me back to L&D (Labor and Delivery) and put me in the triage room, where they would prep me. They had me facing the wall, which was parallel to the left side of the bed. My feet dangled over the bed, while the attending physician sterilized a tray. As I'm waiting for them to start, they informed me that the nurse would be in front of me, while the attending physician would draw 20 CCs of blood from my hand. Then they injected all that blood into my back while I was sitting up. This was extremely painful. The needle that went into my hand was long and my hand already looked like a bruised apple that had been sitting in the sun all day. During the length of my stay, I had numerous blood draws, I.V.'s, and bandages on my hands. This was due to the fact that they have a hard time finding any veins from either arm.

I remember the feeling of the pain and just looking down at my hand and seeing the blood come out. The attending physician handed the syringe to her colleague so he could inject the blood into my back. As he was doing this, he asked me to inform him of any changes that I felt. I told him that I felt a lot of pressure and warmness in my bum. He said this was normal and continued to inject the full 20 CCs into my back. When he was finished, I no longer had a migraine. He then had me lay flat on my back. Then I felt and heard a loud POP!

"Is this normal?"

"Yes, it's the blood moving into place."

I had to wait in L&D for about an hour or so, then the nurse brought me back upstairs where I would be reunited with my son. We would be going home the next day.

During the time of writing this book I did some research about this procedure, and I learned that it was done incorrectly or not with up to-date techniques. According to this website: www.radiology.pitt.edu/epidural-blood-patch.html I should have been lying down on my stomach and a live x-ray machine should've been used for accurate placement. This caused me great concern since the pain and problems I've had to endure since the beginning.

Chapter Nine

Coming Home

Coming home was one of the most stressful events I've ever encountered. I wanted to leave the hospital so badly and informed my husband that I was hoping to get out now.

"Chris, Luke and I are ready to come home."

"Okay, I'll pick up Zoey from daycare after work and head down, as soon as I can."

"Great! Can't wait to see you guys," I told Chris.

I was so excited! When my husband told me he was on his way, I made sure my room was packed up. I laid out an outfit for my son to go home in. I got Luke dressed and started feeding him his bottle. I didn't tighten the cap all the way so it spilled all over Luke and I.

I had to wash his clothes quickly in the sink, wipe myself down, and wait for the slowest nurse to return. The nurse that I had throughout my care was amazing. But there was a shift change on that last day, and I had someone new.

She skipped my doses multiple times. When I asked for something, she'd return hours later. When I asked her if I could be sent home with VNA services, she said she'd add it to the order but never did.

I was told I was being discharged at 11 am. My husband arrived at 7 pm. We waited almost a half hour for the nurse. I had told her my husband was on his way and that she should remove the security bracelet from my son but that didn't happen.

We asked her if we could have some help going down the stairs with our things. We had the baby, my stuff, and my daughter. She declined and said she'd find a volunteer (which is fine). She left and didn't return. My husband had to go find a volunteer that was willing to help us.

I was so angry that my body was in pain. I sat in a wheelchair just wanting to breakdown and cry. I thought, "Why the hell are you a nurse? You don't take care of patients at all." I was tired of her doing a half assed job. What led me to say this about her was when my husband went looking for her, he found her socializing with the other nurses (he could overhear their conversation and it wasn't about helping us).

Getting home was so much work. My husband had to run everything up and come grab both kids while I pulled myself up the stairs. Chris met me halfway because I told him to just stay with the kids. When we reached our apartment, the hell began. I started getting lightning bolt pain from the left side of my buttocks all the way down to my left foot. That foot became more and more numb, until I couldn't feel my last two toes.

I contacted Labor and Delivery and was told that I needed to come in. I grew angry yet again. I felt that the hospital didn't want me to bond with my child. They just wanted to torture me and that’s exactly what they did. When I reached Labor and Delivery, it was roughly 8 pm. I was brought into a room where the Anesthesiologist that did the blood patch examined me.

They wanted to do an M.R.I. They told me it would only be a few hours. It took all night. At 3am, I woke up because I fell asleep while waiting. I asked if I could leave and schedule the M.R.I. They said they wanted me to have it done so they could review it. I informed them that I have two children and a husband that need me. They told me it shouldn’t be much longer.

I went back to sleep and woke up at 6 am. I informed them that I needed to leave because my husband had to go to work. The doctors kept declining: telling me I needed this done ASAP. I cried to the nurse, telling her that they were stripping me of my rights because as a patient, you have the right to go AMA (against medical advice). I didn’t want to go AMA; I wanted to schedule a time to come back because I couldn’t wait there any longer. It took a full hour of convincing them that they needed to let me go.

I wanted to report this to the hospital but never did. I didn't want to hear how they have to protect the hospital from being sued. I saved myself a phone call (this is an assumption, I don't know what the hospital's protocol is for someone who sends in a complaint). I was sent home with discharge paperwork and never had to sign an AMA form that I can recall.

I became angrier at the hospital I once loved. I felt like the providers that entered my life at this time weren't A students. I felt the hospital needed to hire better people with accurate information. They can't just keep someone from leaving without giving him or her the option of AMA.

One of the nurses that night told me that these doctors do this all the time. They kept saying there's only one M.R.I. machine that's in use for the hospital at night. I later learned that the emergency department has their own M.R.I. machine. There's one on the Bridge building and there are multiple other locations that offer nighttime M.R.I. scans. Those would have been able to take in an emergency scan, and even one of their "sister hospitals" could have handled it if they couldn't. This disappointed me so much because I always wanted to work for this hospital. I had shoulder surgery there in 2011 and my doctor was amazing! Then I met my OB/GYN shortly after and she was amazing as well! I just fell in love with the care I had received.

It changed, but why? I wondered if it was just me or bad luck. Or is the hospital falling short on what's required by law and misusing their resources? Granting that it's a teaching hospital, you're bound to get a couple of mistakes. But not like this.

The hospital where I gave birth to both my children is still a special place to me. This may seem hard to believe with all of my emotions and everything that has happened to me. This has been a learning experience and I value what God has put me through to help me see things differently. These are my thoughts about what happened to me during and after the birth of my son. I still very much love the hospital. My point here is for you to remember to use your voice as a patient. Hospitals see hundreds of people and they're losing sight of the patients. They're not allowing the patient to manage their own care.

During this time, I was diagnosed with a cyst in my back, L5 nerve damage, and lumbar spinal stenosis. These were caused by the spinal procedures. This was one of the hardest things I've had to go through. One, I wasn't planning for this and two, because the pain is unbearable sometimes. It's been an exceptionally agonizing recovery.

Chapter Ten

Physical Therapy for Luke & I

Physical therapy was one of the most difficult stages of recovery after a C-section. I chose a facility that had an aqua therapy option - a more gentle therapy. Starting physical therapy with two kids at home and a husband that needed to get back to work was extremely hard. This caused a lot of stress and tense situations.

At one of my first aqua therapy appointments, they had to have two nurses pick me up out of the pool. The following visits got better and/or worse depending on the day. There was a delay for a week because of insurance issues. The insurance company didn't have enough information to process the prior authorization.

I felt like, "What the hell were you writing while I was in the pool for 30 minutes? Were you working on another patient's chart and decided not to go back to mine?" Meanwhile I went to that one appointment and my appeal was denied because the Plan of Care 485 form was missing from my neurologist. I called the rehab center every other day or so for five weeks before the issue was fixed. They kept telling me it wasn't their problem because they had requested this form over and over via fax. They constantly wanted me to call my neurologist. This made me SO angry. I was doing their job and the office manager was completely rude with no compassion at all.

When I confirmed with my neurologist that the form was faxed over from their end, I decided to contact the office manager's boss because I wasn't dealing with her rudeness any longer. Once I spoke with him, things started to move.

My physical therapist contacted me and said, "It could be up to another twenty-one days before you can be seen." I felt hopeless and powerless. It had already been over six weeks! I felt the medical field let me down once again. I was so frustrated because I have two children that depend on me and I need strength to take care of them and myself.

My story doesn't have to be yours: speak up and do what I did but sooner. Embrace failure, embrace negative inputs, and thrive on both positive feedback and reinforcement. It's those negative aspects that will put you in a tornado of emotions, but you need to step out. You can simply say, "Thank you for showing me that you are terrible. Thank you for doubting me because I rose above it without you and we are doing fantastic!"

Make sure you thank everyone, especially the people that have been the most positive. It turned out to be eight weeks before I would hear from the rehab center regarding my insurance. I was only approved for three visits. After that, the same steps would begin again! I was so discouraged. The office manager told me that since it took so long to get me approved (like it was my fault), that I (not them) need to request a new order from my neurologist. Patients have to realize the care, the treatment they need, and rely on healthcare organizations. If they aren't getting correct treatment, they should move on and find a better facility.

When I worked in the medical field, I knew that there would have been people fired for this incompetence. My physical therapist told me her office would request my documents and that they still hadn't received them even by the time I had left. However, the first few weeks I went there, they said they had my records. They were very incompetent.

I would soon start somewhere new and I absolutely loved it. I had knowledgeable, friendly people working with me. Every time I went into this new rehab facility, I got stronger. It was very modified, so I could work up to where I needed to be. I knew great things were going to come from this.

During my progression at this new physical therapy facility, I have been able to feel the last two of my toes. Most of the time they're burning, but this is still progress. I'm still in consistent pain, but some days are better than others. After not being able to go to the grocery store for 6 months, I have finally been able to return. It was a modified trip but I made it through the entire store with a grocery cart! I didn't go down all the isles, but BABY STEPS!

Luke's physical therapy was going great! We started him off at three months old. After the first two visits, he realized that if he fell asleep, she would leave our house.

"Oh, honey why are you crying? You must need a bottle. Let me get him a bottle and I'll be right back."

"Okay." The physical therapist said.

I gave him a bottle and he fell asleep.

"Well it looks like we won't be getting much done today. Let's set something up for next week."

"Okay, I can do next Wednesday at 3:45 pm."

"Sounds great. You guys are in!"

"Perfect. See you then."

I walked his physical therapist out and then decided to go back into the living room: expecting Luke to be sound asleep. Wouldn't you know, I walked in and his eyes were wide-open as he grinned from ear to ear. It was almost like he was trying to tell me, "Look Mom, I got rid of her. Now we can play and do what I want." I couldn't do anything but grab a photo. I started laughing so hard that I was crying.

The thing that's fantastic about his physical therapy is that they come to your house and you don't have to go anywhere. It makes it very convenient since I have a toddler who has a busy schedule too.

At six months, Luke can partially roll over and stay sitting up for more than five minutes unassisted. He's started to use different cooing to let us know he is happy or angry. There are so many best parts of this! I think my favorite is his laugh.

Having physical therapy for him is great because it will help us maintain his milestones. He has a lot of help, especially from his sister. Zoey absolutely adores Luke! She helps him with his physical therapy as well.

We have a lot against us, but we keep moving forward and making sure that Luke is getting the best care. Some of the milestones he hasn't reached yet but we'll celebrate them when he does! I know he'll be able to!

Chapter Eleven

Conclusion

The transition from just being a couple of kids to raising a family truly has been such a blessing and a learning experience. I've learned not to judge someone by their cover but by the actions, words, and structure of their being. When you are building your family, know that every pregnancy and every journey is going to take you down a different road. But it's a road that you'll walk down together.

The NICU experience from the tour to the actual stay truly made me a better person and more understanding. I know outside sources can make or break you as a person and I have decided to have it make me by overcoming all the negative, hurtful, offensive bologna that I've encountered throughout the years. I'm so happy that I've written this book and allowed people into my life.

I hope my research information and birthing/delivery options help other moms. This is why I'm sharing my story to help other families!

The doctors have made me stronger: the providers that were by my side and even the ones who weren't. Doctors are wonderful people. Even though mistakes can be made, it brings a sort of light that they are human too. This hospital will always hold a special part in my heart. It's the reason I went back to school, the reason I've chosen to write this book, and where I had my babies!

Chapter Twelve

Questions to Ask

Some of these questions will not apply, depending on your situation and what you believe in. I have done a lot of research and came up with additional questions for those seeking more answers. Each situation is unique. One brain abnormality can differ from the next ever so slightly. Some of these questions are in more than one category. This is not medical advice. If you have other questions for your provider, then ask them. These questions are meant to serve as a guideline for you. These are questions I asked and some I wished I knew I could ask.

I saw a quote on Pinterest. The quote was (which is perfect for your journey),

"Life is not about waiting for the storm to pass but to learn how to dance in the rain."

Remember every day is a miracle and it is a blessing in disguise.

Obstetrics

1. Are these tests urgent or are you just looking for more information?

2. Are these tests necessary?

3. What resources do I qualify for? (WIC, Social Security, Hospital vouchers, etc)

4. Who is my case manager? Do I have more than one?

5. Can I use a recorder for each appointment so I can go back and listen to all of the information?

6. If I can't, can I have my case manager with me at every appointment to write down everything that I need to know?

7. Is there a bypass number I can call for after hours, or is it just the OB office number?

8. Can we make all the appointments on the same day so I can cut down on travel?

9. Do you offer daycare for the extra appointments so I can make these?

10. Would it be beneficial for me to hire a Doula?

11. Can I have a private room for the post-partum due to the current situation?

12. How much lab work needs to be done? Can I refuse certain tests?

13. Are there specific times that I need to be on the Post Partum Floor and the NICU?

14. Are there any high-risk doctors that I should see?

15. Do I need bed rest?

16. Can I continue to work?

17. Are there diet restrictions?

18. Can I exercise?

19. What specialist am I going to have to see?

20. Do you have brochures on abortion so I can make an educated decision?

21. What is the law in this state for abortion?

22. Is there a waiver I can sign, to have providers stop asking me to terminate pregnancy if I have decided to continue with my pregnancy?

23. Is a mental health worker available to attend some of these harder appointments?

24. Do I have to wait to hold my baby until the nurse gives me him or her?

25. Is live feed okay? (Setting up IPad to record the baby)

26. Is circumcision allowed in the NICU or does that have to be scheduled at a later time?

27. Does the staff pay close attention to what is written in my birth plan for the aftercare and who can come and see my baby and me?

28. What should I eat and avoid eating during pregnancy (and after) for milk production?

29. If I can't breastfeed, what kind of formula is provided?

30. Do you offer a hospital bag of diapers and formula to go home with?

31. What is the hospital's policy on videotaping birth?

32. Can I request to record birth regardless of what the hospital wants and focus on what I want?

Case Manager/Social Worker

1. What resources do I qualify for? (WIC, Social Security Hospital Vouchers, etc.)

2. Can I use a recorder for each appointment so I can go back and listen to all of the information?

3. If I can't, can I have my case manager with me at every appointment to write down everything that I need to know?

4. Is there a bypass number I can call for after hours, or is it just the OB office number?

5. Can we make all the appointments on the same day so I can cut down on travel?

6. Do you offer daycare for the extra appointments so I can make these?

7. Would it be beneficial for me to hire a Doula?

8. Do you have programs that help cover the costs of a Doula?

9. Can I have a private room for the post-partum due to the current situation?

10. Does the NICU have a "Welcome Packet?"

11. Are there specific times that I need to be on the Post Partum Floor and the NICU?

12. Do you have brochures on abortion so I can make an educated decision?

13. What is the law in this state for abortion?

14. Is there a waiver I can sign to have providers stop asking me to terminate pregnancy if I have decided to continue with my pregnancy?

15. Is a mental health worker available to attend some of these harder appointments?

16. Does the staff pay close attention to what is written in my birth plan for the aftercare and who can come and see my baby and me?

17. If I can't breastfeed, what kind of formula is provided?

18. Do you offer a hospital bag of diapers and formula to go home with?

19. Hospital policy on videotaping birth?

20. Can I request to record birth regardless of what the hospital wants and focus on what I want?

21. Will this case manager/social worker stay on my case, or do I have to seek a new one at the designated primary care physician?

High Risk Provider

1. Are these tests urgent or are you just looking for more information?

2. Are these tests necessary?

3. Can I use a recorder for each appointment so I can go back and listen to all of the information?

4. If I can't, can I have my case manager with me at every appointment to write down everything that I need to know?

5. Is there a bypass number I can call for after hours, or is it just the OB office number?

6. Can we make all the appointments on the same day so I can cut down on travel?

7. Can I have a private room for the post-partum due to the current situation?

8. How much lab work needs to be done? Can I refuse certain tests?

9. Do I need bed rest?

10. Can I continue to work?

11. Are there diet restrictions?

12. Can I exercise?

13. Do you have brochures on abortions so I can make an educated decision?

14. What is the law in this state for abortions?

15. Is there a waiver I can sign to have providers stop asking me to terminate pregnancy if I have decided to continue with my pregnancy?

16. Is a mental health worker available to attend some of these harder appointments?

17. Do I have to wait to hold my baby until the nurse gives me him or her?

18. Is live feed okay? (Setting up IPad to record the baby)?

19. Is circumcision allowed in the NICU or does that have to be scheduled at a later time?

20. Hospital policy on videotaping birth?

21. Can I request to record birth regardless of what the hospital wants and focus on what I want?

NICU

1. Are these tests urgent or are you just looking for more information?

2. Are these tests necessary?

3. Can I use a recorder for each appointment so I can go back and listen to all of the information?

4. If I can't, can I have my case manager with me at every appointment to write down everything that I need to know?

5. What is the direct number to the NICU?

6. Can we make all the appointments on the same day so I can cut down on the travel?

7. How much lab work needs to be done? Can I refuse certain tests?

8. Does the NICU have a "Welcome Packet"?

9. Are there specific times that I need to be on the Post Partum Floor and the NICU?

10. Can I sleep in the NICU with my baby?

11. Can I bring flowers or balloons in for my child in the NICU?

12. Can I decorate the NICU?

13. Do I have to wait to hold my baby until the nurse gives me him or her?

14. Is live feed okay? (Setting up IPad to record the baby)?

15. Do we know or expect the baby to be in here for how many days?

16. Is circumcision allowed in the NICU or does that have to be scheduled at a later time?

17. Can I go with my baby to the tests, like the EEG, M.R.I. and/or Ultrasounds?

18. Will the nurse call me if there are any changes?

19. Do you complete all the tests while we are here or do we have to come back?

20. How many nurses per patient/patients?

21. Does the staff pay close attention to what is written in my birth plan for the aftercare and who can come and see my baby and me?

22. If I can't breastfeed, what kind of formula is provided?

23. Do you offer a hospital bag of diapers and formula to go home with?

Specialist

1. Are these tests urgent or are you just looking for more information?

2. Are these tests necessary?

3. Can I use a recorder for each appointment so I can go back and listen to all of the information?

4. If I can't, can I have my case manager with me at every appointment to write down everything that I need to know?

5. Can we make all the appointments on the same day so I can cut down on the travel?

6. How much lab work needs to be done? Can I refuse certain tests?

7. Do I need bed rest?

8. Can I continue to work?

9. Are there diet restrictions?

10. Can I exercise?

11. Is live feed okay? (Setting up IPad to record the baby)?

Ultrasound Technician and Radiologist

1. Are these tests urgent or are you just looking for more information?

2. Are these tests necessary?

3. Can I use a recorder for each appointment so I can go back and listen to all of the information?

4. If I can't, can I have my case manager with me at every appointment to write down everything that I need to know?

5. Can we make all the appointments on the same day so I can cut down on the travel?

6. Is live feed okay? (Setting up IPad to record the baby)?

Dedications

My husband, Chris, you have been fantastic through this whole thing. Granted we have had our ups and downs because of what we've dealt with, which were a lot of different emotions and information. Everyone deals with his or her emotions differently and that's okay because that's what makes us who we are. While he worked during the day I took care of the kids, made sure everyone was okay, and brought our son to his doctor's appointments. I would take our daughter Zoey to daycare before I had to go into the hospital with our son. Chris would come home and I would switch with him, then he would take the kids,while I would run into our bedroom and do homework. I was doing Photography at the time, so I had to do a lot of post-production work. I sometimes would run out to do errands just to escape the house. I would stay up until 12:30 or 1 o'clock every night and still wake up early. Chris was great and he would allow me to sleep in sometimes. When I brought our son home in the beginning, I would get up with Luke. That was until he started acting like it was party time for mommy at 2:30 am, and that was not going to happen. So my husband started taking him. My husband and I didn't always get our time, but that's okay because we still had each other. Chris has been so great for me trying to find myself again. I always reached out for people to take care of by donating time to volunteer, make knitted items, and so forth. Chris, I know you are reading this and I love you so much. You mean the world to the kids and me! You helped me through so much!

To my daughter Zoey!! I love you baby girl! You have been amazing since the day I found out that I was pregnant with you! You have shown me how to love, be patient, and to give more. You brighten up my world and you always wipe my tears when

I'm hurting! I couldn't thank God enough for giving me such a perfect daughter! You mean the world to me and I'm sure our bond will grow stronger and stronger everyday! I LOVE YOU ZOEY!

To my son Luke! Damn dude! Since the beginning you have always had us worried, but you've proved everyone wrong by doing so well! You are my miracle baby and you have my heart wrapped around your finger! If it weren't for you, I would of never wanted to go down this path. You've shown me how to use my passion in loving to care for others in a whole new light. I love you so much Luke and I can't wait to see what you'll do when you get older.

My other rock is my dearest friend and cousin Laura. She has been my sound, she has been my reasoning, and she has been my backbone. She made me believe in my strength again. She taught me to be stronger and that life may throw you lemons, but you got to stand up and embrace those lemons. She would be my late night reasoning. When I did not want to discuss my thoughts and worries with Chris, I would just call her. She always answered and always made sure I was okay. She reached out, every single day or every other day. She made me reach the skies with all of her love and believed in me to be both caring when needed as well as myself. She's my person. I cannot thank her enough because words cannot describe the love I have for her. Being able to have a friend like this is once in a lifetime. She brought the laughter back in me and the belief that I could conquer the task at hand.

I LOVE YOU LAURA!

Other people that were there and I want to personally thank is, Staci M. for always being my best friend: especially after 25 years! When I told Staci about Luke, she said that no matter what it is, she would love Luke no matter what: assuring that we would pull through this. This is the type of person you want! We have had some really great times and I am so thankful you are the Godmother to both of my babies! I am so glad that we have made it through so much and that you have helped me conquer this chapter in my life! I LOVE YOU STACI! Thank you for always coming to everything and making me feel special!

Mike B, what can I say about this sassy individual? (smiley face) I have known him for a long time: he is one of my greatest friends. He is someone that I could call while being a complete ass, and he would tell me that I was being one. We have had no filter and our friendship has really blossomed over the years. We have had our moments, but he stayed with my husband in the nursery and the NICU for each one of my kids. This was all while I could not be there! He is the Godfather to my babies and I couldn't think of any better person for the role. I love you MIKE (of course like a brother, just from a different mother and father LOL)!

I would love to thank both my sister Ashley and my brother Ian because they have always kept me in check. They are always the best calls (when they happen LOL), and they are the best visits. Ashley and Ian have always been there (I would like to think it was not forced LOL). They give me true sibling love with no emotional worries. My husband, kids, and I can be ourselves around them. They do judge us from time to time but they still love us! You guys mean the world to me and I believe in you guys! I love you guys!

I also would love to thank my Grandma Ruth for being the soundboard to my thoughts. Zoey is her 15th great grandchild and Luke is her 16th great grandchild and she loves them so much. She showers that love on Chris, the kids and I! She is always there to be kind, always willing to give you advice if you ask, and always putting a smile on my face! I love you Grandma!

I would love to thank my parents Tom and Pat for being there, babysitting, and helping out with the kids when we needed it. Also for just doing what we ask of them. It makes it easier when you have people that understand your beliefs and not try to change them into their views. I love you guys!

A major thank you to Amy P. Girl, if it weren't for you, I have no idea what I would do! Thank you for taking Zoey in your daycare while I went to all those late nights when we were driving in and out of the city. Thank you for always making sure Zoey had an amazing day and that she loves you! You have cried and laughed with me throughout my whole pregnancy and I needed that. I needed to know my daughter was safe and having fun! Love you Amy!

School is tough with two children. I had started school just before my daughter turned one. A previous client of mine whose wedding I photographed pointed me in the direction to school.

She got me all setup and ready to go at Southern New Hampshire University for Business Administration with the concentration of Healthcare Administration and Nonprofit Management. I had a few advisors before I was ultimately sent to the one that has stuck with me almost since the beginning. We kept in contact during each term/semester and she was one of the first few people with whom I shared the news of my pregnancy! She was so very excited for me and that my school adventure will get better. She was there for me as my life went south in October. Sometimes I just needed someone to talk to and she would listen. When I had academic issues, I made sure that I sent her emails and phone calls. She did the same. Some terms/semesters were better than others and I maintained an A-B average. I was able to get an invitation from the National Society of Leadership and Success a year and a half after starting school because of my 3.6 GPA and I am more than blessed for this to happen. I made sure to tell my advisor and she wasn't screaming, but yelling with excitement. Her excitement made me feel that much better. I've worked so hard and come so far. She is the best advisor in the world that I've ever had to deal with and she has cheered me on every step of the way. From every doctor's appointment and M.R.I. for my son to my school, she was just a fantastic person. I can't say enough how much she means to me and I hope she reads this someday and says "wow, maybe we'll become friends after all of this." She was my rock for both school and life. I love how I have inspired her and other students to stay in school even when life is tough. Thank you so much Mackenzie!

I want to thank Amy W. If it weren't for you, I do not know how I would be able to make it through the NICU tour! I know we have only known each other for a short time, but you were my rock for that appointment. You kept my mind busy and worry free. It was so easy talking to you! I hope we can form a friendship in the future!

Thank you to Natalie! Even though I've only known you for a short period of time, thank you for pushing me and giving me a better quality of life! Thank you for opening my eyes and heart: allowing such great conversations to develop! I really enjoy our talks and hopefully maybe one day we can get the kids together for a play date or a mommy's night out!

Resources

These are some of the New England Hospitals. I have done collective research on different disabilities and added some resources for others with different needs.

Epilepsy Foundation https://www.epilepsy.com/

Service Dog Project, https://www.servicedogproject.org/

Case Managers at your hospital

Some of my local hospitals' main phone numbers

Boston Children's Hospital 617-355-6000

Massachusetts General Hospital 617-726-2000

Beth Israel Deaconess Hospital 617-667-7000

Brigham & Women's Hospital 617-732-5500

Anna Jaques Hospital 978-463-1000

Lawrence General Hospital 978-683-4000

Holy Family Hospital in Methuen 978-687-0151

Hanger Clinic for helmets http://hangerclinic.com/Pages/default.aspx

Social Security https://www.ssa.gov/

Thom Pentucket Child & Family Services, Early Intervention http://www.thomchild.org/

Helmet Bling https://www.blingyourband.com/

Support groups on Facebook

Children's National Health System https://childrensnational.org/choose-childrens/conditions-and-treatments/fetal-carepregnancy/agenesis-of-the-corpus-callosum

National Organization of Rare Disorders https://rarediseases.org/rare-diseases/agenesis-of-corpus-callosum/

National Organization Disorders of the Corpus Callosum https://nodcc.org/corpus-callosum-disorders/faq/

CDC https://www.cdc.gov/epilepsy/index.html

Owlet Monitor https://owletcare.com

Parking Vouchers, at Boston Hospital, ASK FOR THEM!

PMG Organization https://pmgawareness.org/

Medical Definitions. Retrieved From: https://www.online-medical-dictionary.org/

U.S. National Library of Medicine. Retrieved From: https://ghr.nlm.nih.gov/condition/polymicrogyria#genes

Definitions

- **Genetic Counseling** -"An educational process that provides information and advice to individuals or families about a genetic condition that may affect them. The purpose is to help individuals make informed decisions about marriage, reproduction, and other health management issues based on information about the genetic disease, the available diagnostic tests, and management programs. Psychosocial support is usually offered."
- **Abortions** are the "Intentional removal of a fetus from the uterus by any of a number of techniques. (POPLINE, 1978)"
- **C-Section**, also known as caesarean section- "Extraction of the fetus by means of abdominal Hysterotomy"

- **Hysterotomy** is "An incision in the uterus, performed through either the abdomen or the vagina."
- **NICU**-A neonatal intensive care unit (**NICU**), also known as an intensive care nursery (ICN), is an intensive care unit specializing in the care of ill or premature newborn infants.
- **Epilepsy** is a neurological disorder marked by sudden recurrent episodes of sensory disturbance, loss of consciousness, or convulsions, associated with abnormal electrical activity in the brain.
- **Seizures** is 1: a sudden attack (as of disease) especially: the physical manifestations (as convulsions, sensory disturbances, or loss of consciousness) resulting from abnormal electrical discharges in the brain (as in **epilepsy**) 2: an abnormal electrical discharge in the brain.

- **Disabilities** 1: the condition of being **disabled**. 2: limitation in the ability to pursue an occupation because of physical or mental **impairment**.
- **Corpus Callosum**- Agenesis of the **corpus callosum**: A congenital abnormality (a birth defect) in which there is partial or complete absence (agenesis) of the **corpus callosum**, the area of the brain which connects the two cerebral hemispheres (the two halves of the brain).
- **PMG- Polymicrogyria** (**PMG**), is a condition characterized by abnormal development of the brain before birth. ... The surface of the brain normally has many ridges or folds, called gyri. In children born with Polymicrogyria, the brain develops too many folds, and the folds are unusually small.
- **Frontal Lobe** is the part of each hemisphere of the brain located behind the forehead that serves to

regulate and mediate the higher intellectual functions. The **frontal lobes** are important for controlling thoughts, reasoning, and behaviors.

- **Interhemispheric Cyst- Cystic** collection located in the **interhemispheric** fissure, with or without communication with the ventricular system. ... The presence of choroid plexus tissue (originating from the third ventricle) is responsible for the cerebrospinal fluid content of the **cyst**.
- **Third Ventricle** is one cavity in a system of four communicating cavities within the brain that are continuous with the central canal that contains the spinal cord
- **Anesthesiologist** is the field of **Anesthesiology** refers to the branch of **medicine** that studies how to suppress the perception of pain and sensation in the brain.

- **Spinal Block** is a form of regional **anesthesia** involving the injection of a local anaesthetic into the subarachnoid space, generally through a fine needle, usually 9 cm (3.5 in) long.
- **Epidural** is Outside the dura, the outermost, toughest, and most fibrous of the three membranes (meninges) covering the brain and the spinal cord.
- **Catheter** is a hollow flexible tube for **insertion** into a body cavity, duct, or vessel to allow the passage of fluids or distend a passageway. Its uses include the drainage of urine from the bladder through the urethra or **insertion** through a blood vessel into the heart for diagnostic purposes.
- **APGAR Score** is an index used to evaluate the condition of a newborn infant based on a rating of 0, 1, or 2 for each of the five characteristics of color, heart rate, response to stimulation of the sole of the

foot, muscle tone, and respiration with 10 being a perfect **score**.

- **Blood Patch** is a surgical procedure that uses autologous **blood** in order to close one or many holes in the dura mater of the spinal cord, usually as a result of a previous lumbar puncture
- **Pitocin** is used to induce labor or strengthen labor contractions during childbirth, and to control bleeding after childbirth. This **medicine** is also used to stimulate uterine contractions in a woman with an incomplete or threatened miscarriage.
- **Preemie** is a baby born before 37 weeks of gestation have passed.
- **Abnormalities** is Outside the expected norm, or uncharacteristic of a particular patient.
- **Stillborn** is typically defined as fetal death at or after 20 to 28 weeks of pregnancy. It results in a baby born

without signs of life. ... The term is in contrast to miscarriage, which is an early pregnancy loss, and live birth where the baby is born alive, even if it dies shortly after.

- **Circumference** is the outer boundary, especially of a circular area.
- **Breech** is 1: the hind end of the body: buttocks. 2: breech presentation also: a fetus that is presented at the uterine cervix buttocks or legs first.

About the Author

I've lived in Massachusetts my whole life. I live with my husband and children and wanted to share my story. I'm hoping to help families like ours one day. During this time I've been working towards my Bachelors in Business Administration in Nonprofit Management and Healthcare Administration. I've accomplished Medical Assisting School and I'm a part of the National Society of Leadership and Success.

I'm also hoping to do big things in the future and this is the start of something great. I used to love photographing and to go on snowboarding and day trips. Being in physical therapy, I hope I can do these activities to the fullest again! I hope to start a foundation to help families that go through devastating events like this!

Lots of Love,

Sam

Made in the USA
Middletown, DE
03 March 2019